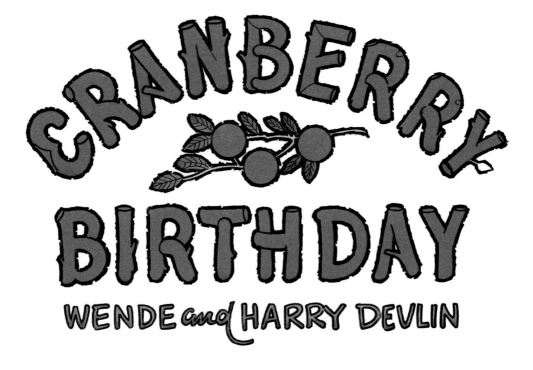

CRANBERRY BIRTHDAY

WENDE and HARRY DEVLIN

ALADDIN BOOKS

Macmillan Publishing Company   New York

Maxwell Macmillan Canada   Toronto

Maxwell Macmillan International
New York   Oxford   Singapore   Sydney

First Aladdin Books edition 1993
Copyright © 1988 by Wende Devlin and Harry Devlin

Aladdin Books
Macmillan Publishing Company
866 Third Avenue
New York, NY 10022

Maxwell Macmillan Canada, Inc.
1200 Eglinton Avenue East
Suite 200
Don Mills, Ontario M3C 3N1

Macmillan Publishing Company is part of the Maxwell
Communication Group of Companies.

Printed in Japan

10 9 8 7 6 5 4 3 2 1

A harcover edition of *Cranberry Birthday* is available from Four
Winds Press, Macmillan Publishing Company.

Library of Congress Cataloging-in-Publication Data
Devlin, Wende.
Cranberry birthday / Wende and Harry Devlin.—1st Aladdin
Books ed.
p.   cm.
Summary: On his birthday, Mr. Whiskers has one calamity after
another until the residents of Cranberryport step in to save
the day. Includes a recipe for strawberry cake.
ISBN 0-689-71697-4
[1. Birthdays—Fiction.]   I. Devlin, Harry.   II. Title.
[PZ7.D49875Co   1993]
[E]—dc20   92-23541

For Sebastian Eldridge

"Mr. Whiskers's sister Sarah is coming for his birth-day," announced Maggie. "*He's* cooking!" she said.

"Oh, NO!" cried Grandmother, putting both hands to her head. "Poor Sarah! Do you remember the awful crab fritters and burned chocolate cake we had at his house?"

"A night to forget," Maggie said, smiling.

"Mr. Whiskers needs help," Grandmother decided.

"Let me call the sewing circle and Seth at the store."

Down in his gray cottage by the ocean, Mr. Whiskers hummed as he cleaned his house for his persnickety sister Sarah. He moved fishnets from the couch and lobster traps from the table. He kicked an empty box out the kitchen door. "There! Beautiful!" he said.

Tired and hot, Mr. Whiskers fancied a swim. He thought about the coolness of Cedar Creek. He remembered the rope on the tree to swing into the water. Fresh, cold water!

"I'll get Grandmother and Maggie to pack a lunch and go with me," he chortled to himself. He shooed the moths away from his old striped bathing suit and quickly climbed into it.

"Cedar Creek, here I come," he sang out.

An hour later Maggie, Grandmother, and Mr. Whiskers stood on the sandy banks of Cedar Creek.

"Look!" shouted Mr. Whiskers. "The rope is still here." Grasping it tightly, he turned to Maggie. "When I was a boy I could make the biggest splash in the county."

He looked over the swift water. A touch of fear clutched at him. Wasn't that a big drop for an old sea captain?

Suddenly Maggie called, "Look, Mr. Whiskers! Quick! There's a little dog floating on a log."

He looked and saw a small white dog bobbing in the water above the rapids.

Now Mr. Whiskers didn't have time to be afraid. The log and the dog would soon be carried into the waterfall below. He took a running start, sailed through the air on the rope like a giant bumblebee, and landed with a mighty splash in front of the log. Paddling from behind, he steered the log carefully to shore.

"Wonderful!" cried Maggie with delight.

"You are a hero," said Grandmother, clapping her hands. "A hero."

Mr. Whiskers trailed out of the water, holding the dog close.

"It's just a puppy." Mr. Whiskers allowed the dog to lick his ears and bite his nose. "But isn't he a beauty?"

At lunchtime, he fed the puppy half of his sandwich and chased him through the grass on hands and knees.

"Sarah never let me have a dog," mused Mr. Whiskers aloud. "She thought they brought too much mud in the house."

He sat up straight. "Suffering codfish! I want this dog, Maggie. I'm going to take him home."

"We can't keep him," said Maggie gently. "He has a
tag that gives his owner's name and address. We will
have to return him today."

Mr. Whiskers was quiet on the walk back. He held
the puppy tight in his arms.

"Here," he said gruffly when they reached town.
"*You* take him back. I've got to tend to some lobster
traps."

Maggie went on her way with the puppy.

Cheers, tears, and happiness greeted her when she returned the pup to his owners. They asked to hear every detail of the rescue. They wanted to know all about Mr. Whiskers.

The night passed, and Mr. Whiskers's birthday dawned with a bright sun and a good breeze.

Up early, he stamped about his kitchen sorting recipes. "Should I have crab fritters and chocolate cake?" he wondered.

Around four o'clock, Grandmother looked over the
dunes to Mr. Whiskers's house. She heard a howl.
Then his kitchen window opened suddenly and a bowl
of something sticky came pouring out. Ten minutes
later the back door opened with an explosion of
burned muffins that landed in the bushes. Soon after
came a cloud of smoke, and Mr. Whiskers leaped into
the yard with a charred pan and a small towel on fire.
He turned the garden hose on the whole menu and
collapsed on the back stairs.

"Suffering codfish, I hate birthdays!"

When he looked up again, a parade of his good friends was hiking over the dunes into his backyard, each one carrying a covered dish.

"Happy Birthday, Mr. Whiskers!" "Congratulations!" they cried. Mr. Whiskers began to brighten up.

"Since you forgot to ask us, we came and brought our own dinner," said Grandmother tartly.

"Thanks, old friend," Mr. Whiskers whispered into Grandmother's ear.

When Sarah arrived, she found a linen-covered picnic table with wildflower bouquets. A good supper of steamed clams and cold turkey, salads and muffins covered the table, and there was lemonade for everyone.

"Where's Maggie?" Mr. Whiskers asked suddenly. Grandmother hesitated for a moment. Then she smiled and pointed. Maggie was running down the path with a puppy in her arms—just like the one Mr. Whiskers had rescued!

Maggie was breathless. "He's the last of the litter that the dog you rescued came from. He's yours—a reward."

Mr. Whiskers's eyes were shining, and a beautiful smile reached across his face.

"Suffering codfish, Maggie. He's no bigger than a horseshoe crab."

"Big enough to bring mud into the kitchen," Sarah said primly.

"I hope he brings mud into the kitchen and upstairs on my bed—where he is going to sleep," announced Mr. Whiskers.

Sarah sniffed. "You're impossible!"

Now Grandmother's beautiful pink cake was placed in front of Mr. Whiskers. Everyone joined in to sing "Happy Birthday to You."

Mr. Whiskers closed his eyes blissfully. He knew he would soon have to blow the blazing candles out.

But for once in his life he couldn't think of a single thing in this whole wide world to wish for.

Not one.

Grandmother's Birthday Cake

(Ask Mother to help)

*Note: Cranberries are out of season
on Mr. Whiskers's birthday, so here
is a wonderful strawberry recipe.*

Make one angel food cake following the directions on the package. When cool, slice the cake into two layers.

Filling

2 cups of fresh strawberries (crushed)
½ cup of granulated sugar

Combine the strawberries and sugar, and spread them to cover the bottom cake layer. Place the top cake layer on the filling.

Frosting

1 cup of fresh strawberries
1 cup of granulated sugar
1 egg white

Put the frosting ingredients in a clean bowl and beat with a mixer or eggbeater until the mixture is *very* stiff and every grain of sugar is dissolved. It will take ten minutes or more. Spread the frosting over the top and sides to cover the entire cake.

'Tis a thing of beauty!